PIPER IN THE WOODS

PHILIP K DICK

Earth maintained an important garrison on Asteroid Y-3. Now suddenly it
was imperiled with a biological impossibility—men becoming plants!

"Well, Corporal Westerburg," Doctor Henry Harris said gently, "just why do you think you're a plant?"

As he spoke, Harris glanced down again at the card on his desk. It was from the Base Commander himself, made out in Cox's heavy scrawl: *Doc, this is the lad I told you about. Talk to him and try to find out how he got this delusion. He's from the new Garrison, the new check-station on Asteroid Y-3, and we don't want anything to go wrong there. Especially a silly damn thing like this!*

Harris pushed the card aside and stared back up at the youth across the desk from him. The young man seemed ill at ease and appeared to be avoiding answering the question Harris had put to him. Harris frowned. Westerburg was a good-looking chap, actually handsome in his Patrol uniform, a shock of blond hair over one eye. He was tall, almost six feet, a fine healthy lad, just two years out of Training, according to the card. Born in Detroit. Had measles when he was nine. Interested in jet engines, tennis, and girls. Twenty-six years old.

"Well, Corporal Westerburg," Doctor Harris said again. "Why do you think you're a plant?"

The Corporal looked up shyly. He cleared his throat. "Sir, I *am* a plant, I don't just think so. I've been a plant for several days, now."

"I see." The Doctor nodded. "You mean that you weren't always a plant?"

"No, sir. I just became a plant recently."

"And what were you before you became a plant?"

"Well, sir, I was just like the rest of you."

There was silence. Doctor Harris took up his pen and scratched a few lines, but nothing of importance came. A plant? And such a healthy-looking lad! Harris removed his steel-rimmed glasses and polished them with his handkerchief. He put them on again and leaned back in his chair. "Care for a cigarette, Corporal?"

"No, sir."

The Doctor lit one himself, resting his arm on the edge of the chair. "Corporal, you must realize that there are very few men who become plants, especially on such short notice. I have to admit you are the first person who has ever told me such a thing."

"Yes, sir, I realize it's quite rare."

2

"You can understand why I'm interested, then. When you say you're a plant, you mean you're not capable of mobility? Or do you mean you're a vegetable, as opposed to an animal? Or just what?"

The Corporal looked away. "I can't tell you any more," he murmured. "I'm sorry, sir."

"Well, would you mind telling me *how* you became a plant?"

Corporal Westerburg hesitated. He stared down at the floor, then out the window at the spaceport, then at a fly on the desk. At last he stood up, getting slowly to his feet. "I can't even tell you that, sir," he said.

"You can't? Why not?"

"Because—because I promised not to."

The room was silent. Doctor Harris rose, too, and they both stood facing each other. Harris frowned, rubbing his jaw. "Corporal, just *who* did you promise?"

"I can't even tell you that, sir. I'm sorry."

The Doctor considered this. At last he went to the door and opened it. "All right, Corporal. You may go now. And thanks for your time."

"I'm sorry I'm not more helpful." The Corporal went slowly out and Harris closed the door after him. Then he went across his office to the vidphone. He rang Commander Cox's letter. A moment later the beefy good-natured face of the Base Commander appeared.

"Cox, this is Harris. I talked to him, all right. All I could get is the statement that he's a plant. What else is there? What kind of behavior pattern?"

"Well," Cox said, "the first thing they noticed was that he wouldn't do any work. The Garrison Chief reported that this Westerburg would wander off outside the Garrison and just sit, all day long. Just sit."

"In the sun?"

"Yes. Just sit in the sun. Then at nightfall he would come back in. When they asked why he wasn't working in the jet repair building he told them he had to be out in the sun. Then he said—" Cox hesitated.

"Yes? Said what?"

"He said that work was unnatural. That it was a waste of time. That the only worthwhile thing was to sit and contemplate—outside."

"What then?"

3

"Then they asked him how he got that idea, and then he revealed to them that he had become a plant."

"I'm going to have to talk to him again, I can see," Harris said. "And he's applied for a permanent discharge from the Patrol? What reason did he give?"

"The same, that he's a plant now, and has no more interest in being a Patrolman. All he wants to do is sit in the sun. It's the damnedest thing I ever heard."

"All right. I think I'll visit him in his quarters." Harris looked at his watch. "I'll go over after dinner."

"Good luck," Cox said gloomily. "But who ever heard of a man turning into a plant? We told him it wasn't possible, but he just smiled at us."

"I'll let you know how I make out," Harris said.

Harris walked slowly down the hall. It was after six; the evening meal was over. A dim concept was coming into his mind, but it was much too soon to be sure. He increased his pace, turning right at the end of the hall. Two nurses passed, hurrying by. Westerburg was quartered with a buddy, a man who had been injured in a jet blast and who was now almost recovered. Harris came to the dorm wing and stopped, checking the numbers on the doors.

"Can I help you, sir?" the robot attendant said, gliding up.

"I'm looking for Corporal Westerburg's room."

"Three doors to the right."

Harris went on. Asteroid Y-3 had only recently been garrisoned and staffed. It had become the primary check-point to halt and examine ships entering the system from outer space. The Garrison made sure that no dangerous bacteria, fungus, or what-not arrived to infect the system. A nice asteroid it was, warm, well-watered, with trees and lakes and lots of sunlight. And the most modern Garrison in the nine planets. He shook his head, coming to the third door. He stopped, raising his hand and knocking.

"Who's there?" sounded through the door.

"I want to see Corporal Westerburg."

The door opened. A bovine youth with horn-rimmed glasses looked out, a book in his hand. "Who are you?"

"Doctor Harris."

"I'm sorry, sir. Corporal Westerburg is asleep."

"Would he mind if I woke him up? I want very much to talk to him." Harris peered inside. He could see a neat room, with a desk, a rug and lamp, and two bunks. On one of

4

the bunks was Westerburg, lying face up, his arms folded across his chest, his eyes tightly closed.

"Sir," the bovine youth said, "I'm afraid I can't wake him up for you, much as I'd like to."

"You can't? Why not?"

"Sir, Corporal Westerburg won't wake up, not after the sun sets. He just won't. He can't be wakened."

"Cataleptic? Really?"

"But in the morning, as soon as the sun comes up, he leaps out of bed and goes outside. Stays the whole day."

"I see," the Doctor said. "Well, thanks anyhow." He went back out into the hall and the door shut after him. "There's more to this than I realized," he murmured. He went on back the way he had come.

It was a warm sunny day. The sky was almost free of clouds and a gentle wind moved through the cedars along the bank of the stream. There was a path leading from the hospital building down the slope to the stream. At the stream a small bridge led over to the other side, and a few patients were standing on the bridge, wrapped in their bathrobes, looking aimlessly down at the water.

It took Harris several minutes to find Westerburg. The youth was not with the other patients, near or around the bridge. He had gone farther down, past the cedar trees and out onto a strip of bright meadow, where poppies and grass grew everywhere. He was sitting on the stream bank, on a flat grey stone, leaning back and staring up, his mouth open a little. He did not notice the Doctor until Harris was almost beside him.

"Hello," Harris said softly.

Westerburg opened his eyes, looking up. He smiled and got slowly to his feet, a graceful, flowing motion that was rather surprising for a man of his size. "Hello, Doctor. What brings you out here?"

"Nothing. Thought I'd get some sun."

"Here, you can share my rock." Westerburg moved over and Harris sat down gingerly, being careful not to catch his trousers on the sharp edges of the rock. He lit a cigarette and gazed silently down at the water. Beside him, Westerburg had resumed his strange position, leaning back, resting on his hands, staring up with his eyes shut tight.

"Nice day," the Doctor said.

"Yes."

"Do you come here every day?"

5

"Yes."

"You like it better out here than inside."

"I can't stay inside," Westerburg said.

"You can't? How do you mean, 'can't'?"

"You would die without *air*, wouldn't you?" the Corporal said.

"And you'd die without sunlight?"

Westerburg nodded.

"Corporal, may I ask you something? Do you plan to do this the rest of your life, sit out in the sun on a flat rock? Nothing else?"

Westerburg nodded.

"How about your job? You went to school for years to become a Patrolman. You wanted to enter the Patrol very badly. You were given a fine rating and a first-class position. How do you feel, giving all that up? You know, it won't be easy to get back in again. Do you realize that?"

"I realize it."

"And you're really going to give it all up?"

"That's right."

Harris was silent for a while. At last he put his cigarette out and turned toward the youth. "All right, let's say you give up your job and sit in the sun. Well, what happens, then? Someone else has to do the job instead of you. Isn't that true? The job has to be done, *your* job has to be done. And if you don't do it someone else has to."

"I suppose so."

"Westerburg, suppose everyone felt the way you do? Suppose everyone wanted to sit in the sun all day? What would happen? No one would check ships coming from outer space. Bacteria and toxic crystals would enter the system and cause mass death and suffering. Isn't that right?"

"If everyone felt the way I do they wouldn't be going into outer space."

"But they have to. They have to trade, they have to get minerals and products and new plants."

"Why?"

"To keep society going."

6

"Why?"

"Well—" Harris gestured. "People couldn't live without society."

Westerburg said nothing to that. Harris watched him, but the youth did not answer.

"Isn't that right?" Harris said.

"Perhaps. It's a peculiar business, Doctor. You know, I struggled for years to get through Training. I had to work and pay my own way. Washed dishes, worked in kitchens. Studied at night, learned, crammed, worked on and on. And you know what I think, now?"

"What?"

"I wish I'd become a plant earlier."

Doctor Harris stood up. "Westerburg, when you come inside, will you stop off at my office? I want to give you a few tests, if you don't mind."

"The shock box?" Westerburg smiled. "I knew that would be coming around. Sure, I don't mind."

Nettled, Harris left the rock, walking back up the bank a short distance. "About three, Corporal?"

The Corporal nodded.

Harris made his way up the hill, to the path, toward the hospital building. The whole thing was beginning to become more clear to him. A boy who had struggled all his life. Financial insecurity. Idealized goal, getting a Patrol assignment. Finally reached it, found the load too great. And on Asteroid Y-3 there was too much vegetation to look at all day. Primitive identification and projection on the flora of the asteroid. Concept of security involved in immobility and permanence. Unchanging forest.

He entered the building. A robot orderly stopped him almost at once. "Sir, Commander Cox wants you urgently, on the vidphone."

"Thanks." Harris strode to his office. He dialed Cox's letter and the Commander's face came presently into focus. "Cox? This is Harris. I've been out talking to the boy. I'm beginning to get this lined up, now. I can see the pattern, too much load too long. Finally gets what he wants and the idealization shatters under the—"

"Harris!" Cox barked. "Shut up and listen. I just got a report from Y-3. They're sending an express rocket here. It's on the way."

"An express rocket?"

"Five more cases like Westerburg. All say they're plants! The Garrison Chief is worried as hell. Says we *must* find out what it is or the Garrison will fall apart, right away. Do you get me, Harris? Find out what it is!"

"Yes, sir," Harris murmured. "Yes, sir."

By the end of the week there were twenty cases, and all, of course, were from Asteroid Y-3.

Commander Cox and Harris stood together at the top of the hill, looking gloomily down at the stream below. Sixteen men and four women sat in the sun along the bank, none of them moving, none speaking. An hour had gone by since Cox and Harris appeared, and in all that time the twenty people below had not stirred.

"I don't get it," Cox said, shaking his head. "I just absolutely don't get it. Harris, is this the beginning of the end? Is everything going to start cracking around us? It gives me a hell of a strange feeling to see those people down there, basking away in the sun, just sitting and basking."

"Who's that man there with the red hair?"

"That's Ulrich Deutsch. He was Second in Command at the Garrison. Now look at him! Sits and dozes with his mouth open and his eyes shut. A week ago that man was climbing, going right up to the top. When the Garrison Chief retires he was supposed to take over. Maybe another year, at the most. All his life he's been climbing to get up there."

"And now he sits in the sun," Harris finished.

"That woman. The brunette, with the short hair. Career woman. Head of the entire office staff of the Garrison. And the man beside her. Janitor. And that cute little gal there, with the bosom. Secretary, just out of school. All kinds. And I got a note this morning, three more coming in sometime today."

Harris nodded. "The strange thing is—they really *want* to sit down there. They're completely rational; they could do something else, but they just don't care to."

"Well?" Cox said. "What are you going to do? Have you found anything? We're counting on you. Let's hear it."

"I couldn't get anything out of them directly," Harris said, "but I've had some interesting results with the shock box. Let's go inside and I'll show you."

"Fine," Cox turned and started toward the hospital. "Show me anything you've got. This is serious. Now I know how Tiberius felt when Christianity showed up in high places."

Harris snapped off the light. The room was pitch black. "I'll run this first reel for you. The subject is one of the best biologists stationed at the Garrison. Robert Bradshaw. He came in yesterday. I got a good run from the shock box because Bradshaw's mind is so highly differentiated. There's a lot of repressed material of a non-rational nature, more than usual."

He pressed a switch. The projector whirred, and on the far wall a three-dimensional image appeared in color, so real that it might have been the man himself. Robert Bradshaw was a man of fifty, heavy-set, with iron grey hair and a square jaw. He sat in the chair calmly, his hands resting on the arms, oblivious to the electrodes attached to his neck and wrist. "There I go," Harris said. "Watch."

His film-image appeared, approaching Bradshaw. "Now, Mr. Bradshaw," his image said, "this won't hurt you at all, and it'll help us a lot." The image rotated the controls on the shock box. Bradshaw stiffened, and his jaw set, but otherwise he gave no sign. The image of Harris regarded him for a time and then stepped away from the controls.

"Can you hear me, Mr. Bradshaw?" the image asked.

"Yes."

"What is your name?"

"Robert C. Bradshaw."

"What is your position?"

"Chief Biologist at the check-station on Y-3."

"Are you there now?"

"No, I'm back on Terra. In a hospital."

"Why?"

"Because I admitted to the Garrison Chief that I had become a plant."

"Is that true? That you are a plant."

"Yes, in a non-biological sense. I retain the physiology of a human being, of course."

"What do you mean, then, that you're a plant?"

"The reference is to attitudinal response, to Weltanschauung."

"Go on."

"It is possible for a warm-blooded animal, an upper primate, to adopt the psychology of a plant, to some extent."

"Yes?"

"I refer to this."

9

"And the others? They refer to this also?"

"Yes."

"How did this occur, your adopting this attitude?"

Bradshaw's image hesitated, the lips twisting. "See?" Harris said to Cox. "Strong conflict. He wouldn't have gone on, if he had been fully conscious."

"I—"

"Yes?"

"I was taught to become a plant."

The image of Harris showed surprise and interest. "What do you mean, you were *taught* to become a plant?"

"They realized my problems and taught me to become a plant. Now I'm free from them, the problems."

"Who? Who taught you?"

"The Pipers."

"Who? The Pipers? Who are the Pipers?"

There was no answer.

"Mr. Bradshaw, who are the Pipers?"

After a long, agonized pause, the heavy lips parted. "They live in the woods...."

Harris snapped off the projector, and the lights came on. He and Cox blinked. "That was all I could get," Harris said. "But I was lucky to get that. He wasn't supposed to tell, not at all. That was the thing they all promised not to do, tell who taught them to become plants. The Pipers who live in the woods, on Asteroid Y-3."

"You got this story from all twenty?"

"No." Harris grimaced. "Most of them put up too much fight. I couldn't even get *this* much from them."

Cox reflected. "The Pipers. Well? What do you propose to do? Just wait around until you can get the full story? Is that your program?"

"No," Harris said. "Not at all. I'm going to Y-3 and find out who the Pipers are, myself."

The small patrol ship made its landing with care and precision, its jets choking into final silence. The hatch slid back and Doctor Henry Harris found himself staring out at a

10

field, a brown, sun-baked landing field. At the end of the field was a tall signal tower. Around the field on all sides were long grey buildings, the Garrison check-station itself. Not far off a huge Venusian cruiser was parked, a vast green hulk, like an enormous lime. The technicians from the station were swarming all over it, checking and examining each inch of it for lethal life-forms and poisons that might have attached themselves to the hull.

"All out, sir," the pilot said.

Harris nodded. He took hold of his two suitcases and stepped carefully down. The ground was hot underfoot, and he blinked in the bright sunlight. Jupiter was in the sky, and the vast planet reflected considerable sunlight down onto the asteroid.

Harris started across the field, carrying his suitcases. A field attendant was already busy opening the storage compartment of the patrol ship, extracting his trunk. The attendant lowered the trunk into a waiting dolly and came after him, manipulating the little truck with bored skill.

As Harris came to the entrance of the signal tower the gate slid back and a man came forward, an older man, large and robust, with white hair and a steady walk.

"How are you, Doctor?" he said, holding his hand out. "I'm Lawrence Watts, the Garrison Chief."

They shook hands. Watts smiled down at Harris. He was a huge old man, still regal and straight in his dark blue uniform, with his gold epaulets sparkling on his shoulders.

"Have a good trip?" Watts asked. "Come on inside and I'll have a drink fixed for you. It gets hot around here, with the Big Mirror up there."

"Jupiter?" Harris followed him inside the building. The signal tower was cool and dark, a welcome relief. "Why is the gravity so near Terra's? I expected to go flying off like a kangaroo. Is it artificial?"

"No. There's a dense core of some kind to the asteroid, some kind of metallic deposit. That's why we picked this asteroid out of all the others. It made the construction problem much simpler, and it also explains why the asteroid has natural air and water. Did you see the hills?"

"The hills?"

"When we get up higher in the tower we'll be able to see over the buildings. There's quite a natural park here, a regular little forest, complete with everything you'd want. Come in here, Harris. This is my office." The old man strode at quite a clip, around the corner and into a large, well-furnished apartment. "Isn't this pleasant? I intend to make my last year here as amiable as possible." He frowned. "Of course, with Deutsch gone, I may be here forever. Oh, well." He shrugged. "Sit down, Harris."

"Thanks." Harris took a chair, stretching his legs out. He watched Watts as he closed the door to the hall. "By the way, any more cases come up?"

11

"Two more today," Watts was grim. "Makes almost thirty, in all. We have three hundred men in this station. At the rate it's going—"

"Chief, you spoke about a forest on the asteroid. Do you allow the crew to go into the forest at will? Or do you restrict them to the buildings and grounds?"

Watts rubbed his jaw. "Well, it's a difficult situation, Harris. I have to let the men leave the grounds sometimes. They can *see* the forest from the buildings, and as long as you can see a nice place to stretch out and relax that does it. Once every ten days they have a full period of rest. Then they go out and fool around."

"And then it happens?"

"Yes, I suppose so. But as long as they can see the forest they'll want to go. I can't help it."

"I know. I'm not censuring you. Well, what's your theory? What happens to them out there? What do they do?"

"What happens? Once they get out there and take it easy for a while they don't want to come back and work. It's boondoggling. Playing hookey. They don't want to work, so off they go."

"How about this business of their delusions?"

Watts laughed good-naturedly. "Listen, Harris. You know as well as I do that's a lot of poppycock. They're no more plants than you or I. They just don't want to work, that's all. When I was a cadet we had a few ways to make people work. I wish we could lay a few on their backs, like we used to."

"You think this is simple goldbricking, then?"

"Don't you think it is?"

"No," Harris said. "They really believe they're plants. I put them through the high-frequency shock treatment, the shock box. The whole nervous system is paralyzed, all inhibitions stopped cold. They tell the truth, then. And they said the same thing—and more."

Watts paced back and forth, his hands clasped behind his back. "Harris, you're a doctor, and I suppose you know what you're talking about. But look at the situation here. We have a garrison, a good modern garrison. We're probably the most modern outfit in the system. Every new device and gadget is here that science can produce. Harris, this garrison is one vast machine. The men are parts, and each has his job, the Maintenance Crew, the Biologists, the Office Crew, the Managerial Staff.

"Look what happens when one person steps away from his job. Everything else begins to creak. We can't service the bugs if no one services the machines. We can't order food to feed the crews if no one makes out reports, takes inventories. We can't direct any kind of activity if the Second in Command decides to go out and sit in the sun all day.

12

"Thirty people, one tenth of the Garrison. But we can't run without them. The Garrison is built that way. If you take the supports out the whole building falls. No one can leave. We're all tied here, and these people know it. They know they have no right to do that, run off on their own. No one has that right anymore. We're all too tightly interwoven to suddenly start doing what we want. It's unfair to the rest, the majority."

Harris nodded. "Chief, can I ask you something?"

"What is it?"

"Are there any inhabitants on the asteroid? Any natives?"

"Natives?" Watts considered. "Yes, there's some kind of aborigines living out there." He waved vaguely toward the window.

"What are they like? Have you seen them?"

"Yes, I've seen them. At least, I saw them when we first came here. They hung around for a while, watching us, then after a time they disappeared."

"Did they die off? Diseases of some kind?"

"No. They just—just disappeared. Into their forest. They're still there, someplace."

"What kind of people are they?"

"Well, the story is that they're originally from Mars. They don't look much like Martians, though. They're dark, a kind of coppery color. Thin. Very agile, in their own way. They hunt and fish. No written language. We don't pay much attention to them."

"I see." Harris paused. "Chief, have you ever heard of anything called—The Pipers?"

"The Pipers?" Watts frowned. "No. Why?"

"The patients mentioned something called The Pipers. According to Bradshaw, the Pipers taught him to become a plant. He learned it from them, a kind of teaching."

"The Pipers. What are they?"

"I don't know," Harris admitted. "I thought maybe you might know. My first assumption, of course, was that they're the natives. But now I'm not so sure, not after hearing your description of them."

"The natives are primitive savages. They don't have anything to teach anybody, especially a top-flight biologist."

Harris hesitated. "Chief, I'd like to go into the woods and look around. Is that possible?"

"Certainly. I can arrange it for you. I'll give you one of the men to show you around."

13

"I'd rather go alone. Is there any danger?"

"No, none that I know of. Except—"

"Except the Pipers," Harris finished. "I know. Well, there's only one way to find them, and that's it. I'll have to take my chances."

"If you walk in a straight line," Chief Watts said, "you'll find yourself back at the Garrison in about six hours. It's a damn small asteroid. There's a couple of streams and lakes, so don't fall in."

"How about snakes or poisonous insects?"

"Nothing like that reported. We did a lot of tramping around at first, but it's grown back now, the way it was. We never encountered anything dangerous."

"Thanks, Chief," Harris said. They shook hands. "I'll see you before nightfall."

"Good luck." The Chief and his two armed escorts turned and went back across the rise, down the other side toward the Garrison. Harris watched them go until they disappeared inside the building. Then he turned and started into the grove of trees.

The woods were very silent around him as he walked. Trees towered up on all sides of him, huge dark-green trees like eucalyptus. The ground underfoot was soft with endless leaves that had fallen and rotted into soil. After a while the grove of high trees fell behind and he found himself crossing a dry meadow, the grass and weeds burned brown in the sun. Insects buzzed around him, rising up from the dry weed-stalks. Something scuttled ahead, hurrying through the undergrowth. He caught sight of a grey ball with many legs, scampering furiously, its antennae weaving.

The meadow ended at the bottom of a hill. He was going up, now, going higher and higher. Ahead of him an endless expanse of green rose, acres of wild growth. He scrambled to the top finally, blowing and panting, catching his breath.

He went on. Now he was going down again, plunging into a deep gully. Tall ferns grew, as large as trees. He was entering a living Jurassic forest, ferns that stretched out endlessly ahead of him. Down he went, walking carefully. The air began to turn cold around him. The floor of the gully was damp and silent; underfoot the ground was almost wet.

He came out on a level table. It was dark, with the ferns growing up on all sides, dense growths of ferns, silent and unmoving. He came upon a natural path, an old stream bed, rough and rocky, but easy to follow. The air was thick and oppressive. Beyond the ferns he could see the side of the next hill, a green field rising up.

Something grey was ahead. Rocks, piled-up boulders, scattered and stacked here and there. The stream bed led directly to them. Apparently this had been a pool of some kind, a stream emptying from it. He climbed the first of the boulders awkwardly, feeling his way up. At the top he paused, resting again.

14

As yet he had had no luck. So far he had not met any of the natives. It would be through them that he would find the mysterious Pipers that were stealing the men away, if such really existed. If he could find the natives, talk to them, perhaps he could find out something. But as yet he had been unsuccessful. He looked around. The woods were very silent. A slight breeze moved through the ferns, rustling them, but that was all. Where were the natives? Probably they had a settlement of some sort, huts, a clearing. The asteroid was small; he should be able to find them by nightfall.

He started down the rocks. More rocks rose up ahead and he climbed them. Suddenly he stopped, listening. Far off, he could hear a sound, the sound of water. Was he approaching a pool of some kind? He went on again, trying to locate the sound. He scrambled down rocks and up rocks, and all around him there was silence, except for the splashing of distant water. Maybe a waterfall, water in motion. A stream. If he found the stream he might find the natives.

The rocks ended and the stream bed began again, but this time it was wet, the bottom muddy and overgrown with moss. He was on the right track; not too long ago this stream had flowed, probably during the rainy season. He went up on the side of the stream, pushing through the ferns and vines. A golden snake slid expertly out of his path. Something glinted ahead, something sparkling through the ferns. Water. A pool. He hurried, pushing the vines aside and stepping out, leaving them behind.

He was standing on the edge of a pool, a deep pool sunk in a hollow of grey rocks, surrounded by ferns and vines. The water was clear and bright, and in motion, flowing in a waterfall at the far end. It was beautiful, and he stood watching, marveling at it, the undisturbed quality of it. Untouched, it was. Just as it had always been, probably. As long as the asteroid existed. Was he the first to see it? Perhaps. It was so hidden, so concealed by the ferns. It gave him a strange feeling, a feeling almost of ownership. He stepped down a little toward the water.

And it was then he noticed her.

The girl was sitting on the far edge of the pool, staring down into the water, resting her head on one drawn-up knee. She had been bathing; he could see that at once. Her coppery body was still wet and glistening with moisture, sparkling in the sun. She had not seen him. He stopped, holding his breath, watching her.

She was lovely, very lovely, with long dark hair that wound around her shoulders and arms. Her body was slim, very slender, with a supple grace to it that made him stare, accustomed as he was to various forms of anatomy. How silent she was! Silent and unmoving, staring down at the water. Time passed, strange, unchanging time, as he watched the girl. Time might even have ceased, with the girl sitting on the rock staring into the water, and the rows of great ferns behind her, as rigid as if they had been painted there.

All at once the girl looked up. Harris shifted, suddenly conscious of himself as an intruder. He stepped back. "I'm sorry," he murmured. "I'm from the Garrison. I didn't mean to come poking around."

She nodded without speaking.

15

"You don't mind?" Harris asked presently.

"No."

So she spoke Terran! He moved a little toward her, around the side of the pool. "I hope you don't mind my bothering you. I won't be on the asteroid very long. This is my first day here. I just arrived from Terra."

She smiled faintly.

"I'm a doctor. Henry Harris." He looked down at her, at the slim coppery body, gleaming in the sunlight, a faint sheen of moisture on her arms and thighs. "You might be interested in why I'm here." He paused. "Maybe you can even help me."

She looked up a little. "Oh?"

"Would you like to help me?"

She smiled. "Yes. Of course."

"That's good. Mind if I sit down?" He looked around and found himself a flat rock. He sat down slowly, facing her. "Cigarette?"

"No."

"Well, I'll have one." He lit up, taking a deep breath. "You see, we have a problem at the Garrison. Something has been happening to some of the men, and it seems to be spreading. We have to find out what causes it or we won't be able to run the Garrison."

He waited for a moment. She nodded slightly. How silent she was! Silent and unmoving. Like the ferns.

"Well, I've been able to find out a few things from them, and one very interesting fact stands out. They keep saying that something called—called The Pipers are responsible for their condition. They say the Pipers taught them—" He stopped. A strange look had flitted across her dark, small face. "Do you know the Pipers?"

She nodded.

Acute satisfaction flooded over Harris. "You do? I was sure the natives would know." He stood up again. "I was sure they would, if the Pipers really existed. Then they do exist, do they?"

"They exist."

Harris frowned. "And they're here, in the woods?"

"Yes."

16

"I see." He ground his cigarette out impatiently. "You don't suppose there's any chance you could take me to them, do you?"

"Take you?"

"Yes. I have this problem and I have to solve it. You see, the Base Commander on Terra has assigned this to me, this business about the Pipers. It has to be solved. And I'm the one assigned to the job. So it's important to me to find them. Do you see? Do you understand?"

She nodded.

"Well, will you take me to them?"

The girl was silent. For a long time she sat, staring down into the water, resting her head against her knee. Harris began to become impatient. He fidgeted back and forth, resting first on one leg and then on the other.

"Well, will you?" he said again. "It's important to the whole Garrison. What do you say?" He felt around in his pockets. "Maybe I could give you something. What do I have...." He brought out his lighter. "I could give you my lighter."

The girl stood up, rising slowly, gracefully, without motion or effort. Harris' mouth fell open. How supple she was, gliding to her feet in a single motion! He blinked. Without effort she had stood, seemingly without *change*. All at once she was standing instead of sitting, standing and looking calmly at him, her small face expressionless.

"Will you?" he said.

"Yes. Come along." She turned away, moving toward the row of ferns.

Harris followed quickly, stumbling across the rocks. "Fine," he said. "Thanks a lot. I'm very interested to meet these Pipers. Where are you taking me, to your village? How much time do we have before nightfall?"

The girl did not answer. She had entered the ferns already, and Harris quickened his pace to keep from losing her. How silently she glided!

"Wait," he called. "Wait for me."

The girl paused, waiting for him, slim and lovely, looking silently back.

He entered the ferns, hurrying after her.

"Well, I'll be damned!" Commander Cox said. "It sure didn't take you long." He leaped down the steps two at a time. "Let me give you a hand."

Harris grinned, lugging his heavy suitcases. He set them down and breathed a sigh of relief. "It isn't worth it," he said. "I'm going to give up taking so much."

17

"Come on inside. Soldier, give him a hand." A Patrolman hurried over and took one of the suitcases. The three men went inside and down the corridor to Harris' quarters. Harris unlocked the door and the Patrolman deposited his suitcase inside.

"Thanks," Harris said. He set the other down beside it. "It's good to be back, even for a little while."

"A little while?"

"I just came back to settle my affairs. I have to return to Y-3 tomorrow morning."

"Then you didn't solve the problem?"

"I solved it, but I haven't *cured* it. I'm going back and get to work right away. There's a lot to be done."

"But you found out what it is?"

"Yes. It was just what the men said. The Pipers."

"The Pipers do exist?"

"Yes." Harris nodded. "They do exist." He removed his coat and put it over the back of the chair. Then he went to the window and let it down. Warm spring air rushed into the room. He settled himself on the bed, leaning back.

"The Pipers exist, all right—in the minds of the Garrison crew! To the crew, the Pipers are real. The crew created them. It's a mass hypnosis, a group projection, and all the men there have it, to some degree."

"How did it start?"

"Those men on Y-3 were sent there because they were skilled, highly-trained men with exceptional ability. All their lives they've been schooled by complex modern society, fast tempo and high integration between people. Constant pressure toward some goal, some job to be done."

"Those men are put down suddenly on an asteroid where there are natives living the most primitive of existence, completely vegetable lives. No concept of goal, no concept of purpose, and hence no ability to plan. The natives live the way the animals live, from day to day, sleeping, picking food from the trees. A kind of Garden-of-Eden existence, without struggle or conflict."

"So? But—"

"Each of the Garrison crew sees the natives and *unconsciously* thinks of his own early life, when he was a child, when *he* had no worries, no responsibilities, before he joined modern society. A baby lying in the sun.

18

"But he can't admit this to himself! He can't admit that he might *want* to live like the natives, to lie and sleep all day. So he invents The Pipers, the idea of a mysterious group living in the woods who trap him, lead him into their kind of life. Then he can blame *them*, not himself. They 'teach' him to become a part of the woods."

"What are you going to do? Have the woods burned?"

"No." Harris shook his head. "That's not the answer; the woods are harmless. The answer is psychotherapy for the men. That's why I'm going right back, so I can begin work. They've got to be made to see that the Pipers are inside them, their own unconscious voices calling to them to give up their responsibilities. They've got to be made to realize that there are no Pipers, at least, not outside themselves. The woods are harmless and the natives have nothing to teach anyone. They're primitive savages, without even a written language. We're seeing a psychological projection by a whole Garrison of men who want to lay down their work and take it easy for a while."

The room was silent.

"I see," Cox said presently. "Well, it makes sense." He got to his feet. "I hope you can do something with the men when you get back."

"I hope so, too," Harris agreed. "And I think I can. After all, it's just a question of increasing their self-awareness. When they have that the Pipers will vanish."

Cox nodded. "Well, you go ahead with your unpacking, Doc. I'll see you at dinner. And maybe before you leave, tomorrow."

"Fine."

Harris opened the door and the Commander went out into the hall. Harris closed the door after him and then went back across the room. He looked out the window for a moment, his hands in his pockets.

It was becoming evening, the air was turning cool. The sun was just setting as he watched, disappearing behind the buildings of the city surrounding the hospital. He watched it go down.

Then he went over to his two suitcases. He was tired, very tired from his trip. A great weariness was beginning to descend over him. There were so many things to do, so terribly many. How could he hope to do them all? Back to the asteroid. And then what?

He yawned, his eyes closing. How sleepy he was! He looked over at the bed. Then he sat down on the edge of it and took his shoes off. So much to do, the next day.

He put his shoes in the corner of the room. Then he bent over, unsnapping one of the suitcases. He opened the suitcase. From it he took a bulging gunnysack. Carefully, he emptied the contents of the sack out on the floor. Dirt, rich soft dirt. Dirt he had collected during his last hours there, dirt he had carefully gathered up.

19

When the dirt was spread out on the floor he sat down in the middle of it. He stretched himself out, leaning back. When he was fully comfortable he folded his hands across his chest and closed his eyes. So much work to do—But later on, of course. Tomorrow. How warm the dirt was....

He was sound asleep in a moment.

Milton Keynes UK
Ingram Content Group UK Ltd.
UKHW040655050923
428087UK00004B/517